To Michelle, Mia and Maren, our three little

• A.A.K & J.A.K

To Pauline, Elena, Greta and Bianca, my queen and princesses for life

• D.F.

Copyright © 2022 by Lightspan Ent, LLC.

All rights reserved. Published in the United States by Lightspan Ent., LLC. No part of this book may be reproduced or transmitted in any form or by any means, electronic or mechanical, including photocopying, recording, or by any information storage and retrieval system, without written permission from Lightspan Ent, LLC.

For further information please contact:

**Lightspan Ent. LLC,
4532 Kraft Ave.,
N. Hollywood, CA 91602**

VISIT www.**lightspanent**.com

A long time ago, in a far away kingdom, a Princess lived in a Royal Castle.

Even though she had a lot of toys,
a lot of pretty things,
and lived with a lot of people,
she was very lonely.

Her father,
the King,
was very busy...
being a King.

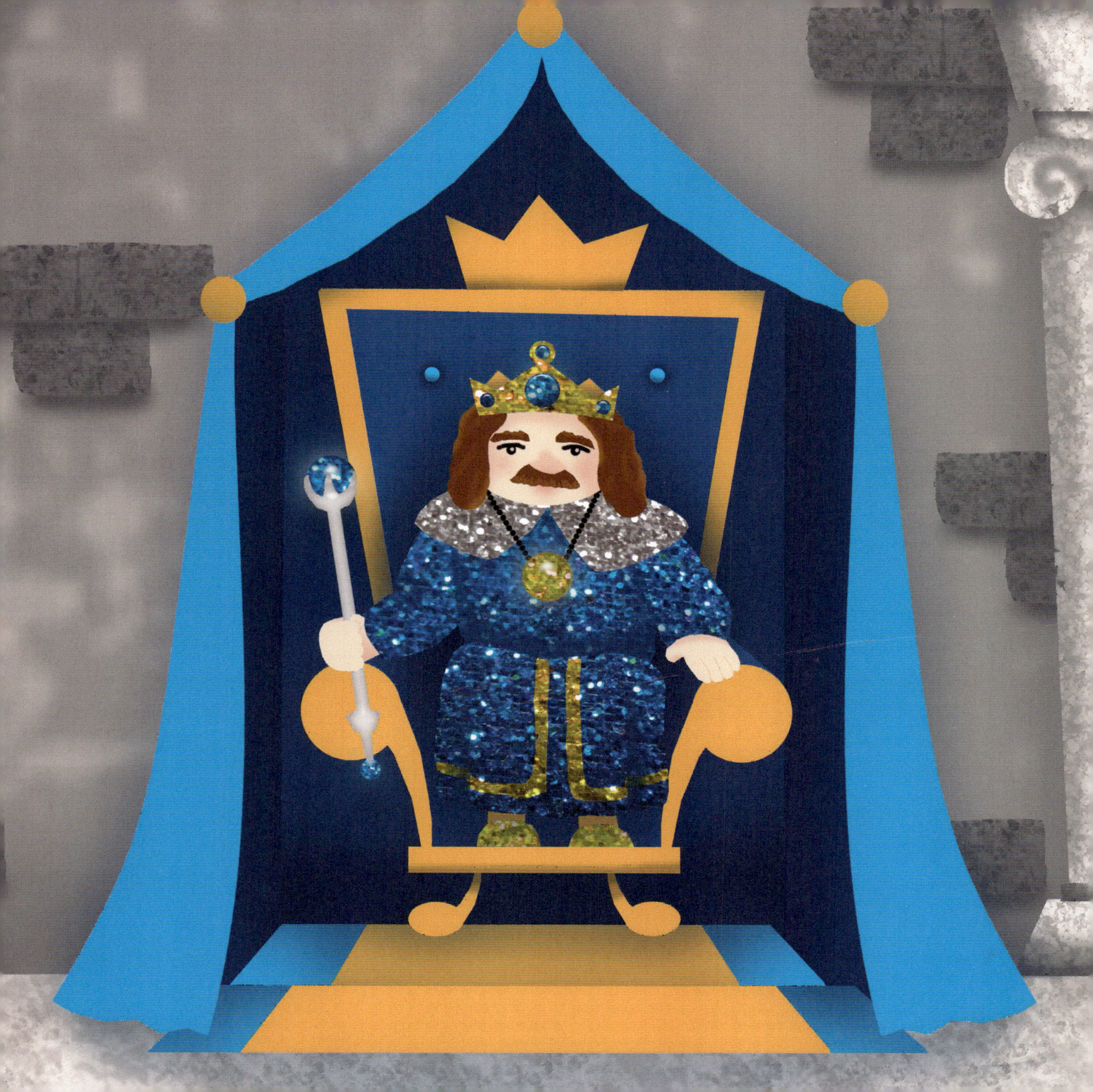

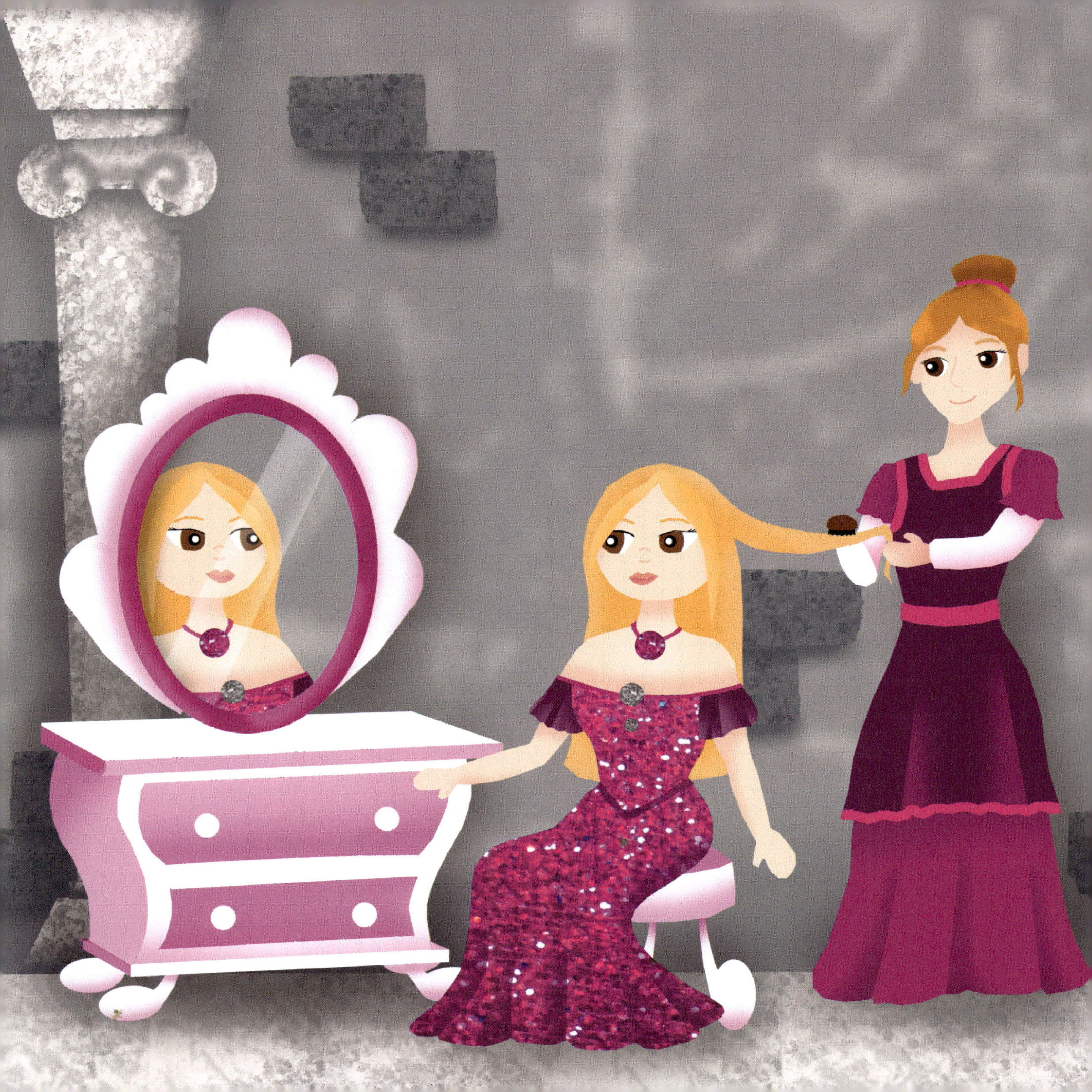

Her mother, the Queen, was also very busy... being a Queen.

Her brother,
the Prince,
was busy
as well...
being a Prince.

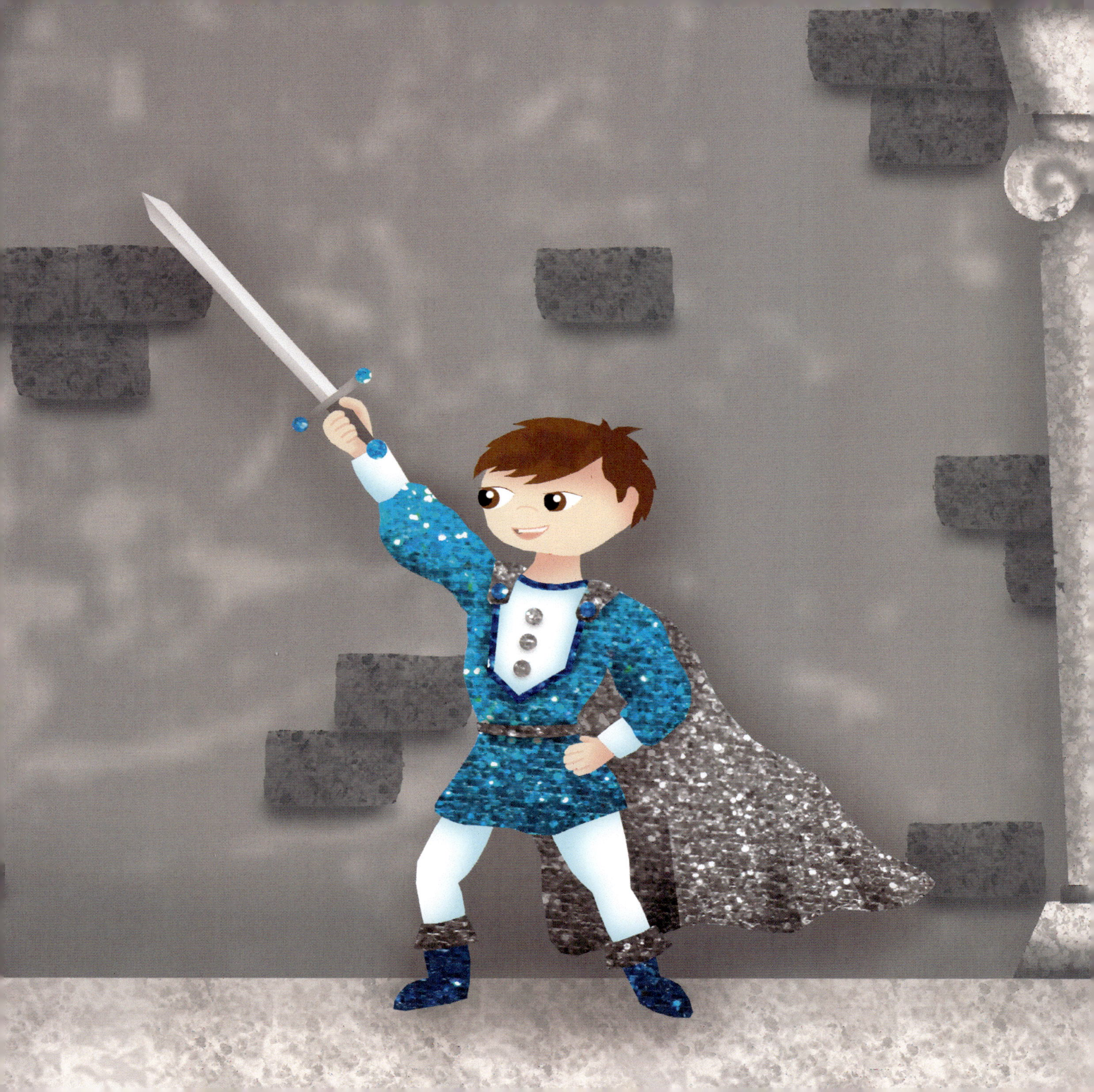

There were a lot of servants in the castle, but they were no fun to play with.

She needed a friend.

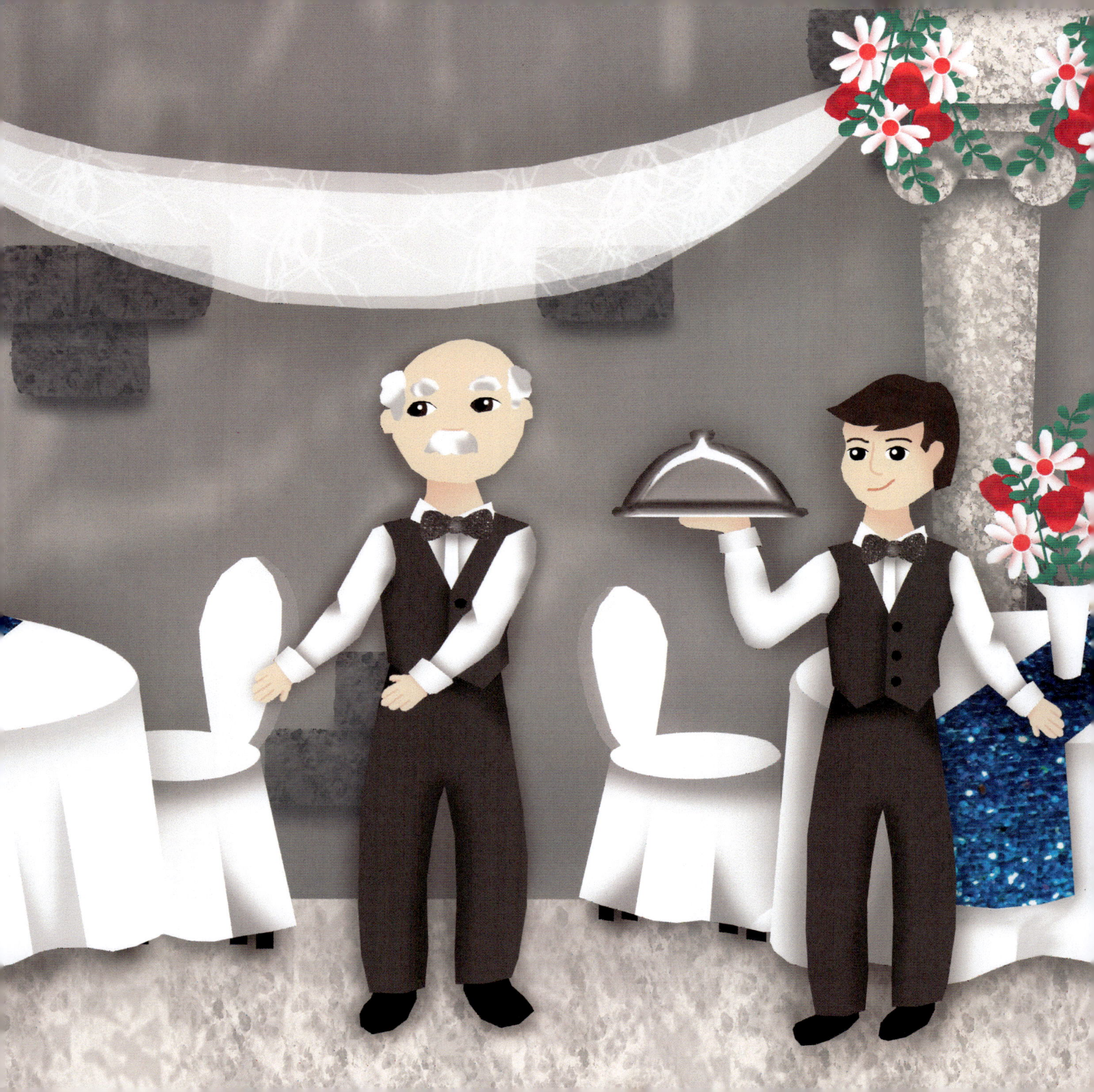

ROYAL

One day, she visited the Royal Zoo.

ZOO

There were
so many animals.
They all seemed to
have such fun together.

ROYAL

Zoo

The Princess wondered, "Could a zoo animal be my friend?"

First, the Princess visited the monkeys.

"Monkeys have hands," she thought,
as she watched them swing from the trees.

"They could play with toys in my Royal Playroom.
Maybe they could be my friends."

But the monkeys were too silly. They did not want a princess friend.

The Princess was sad.

Next the Princess visited the zebras.

"The zebras have long legs," she thought as she watched them frolic in the grass.

"They could race through my Royal Field. Maybe they could be my friends."

But the zebras
were too fast.
They did not want
a princess friend.

The Princess was sad.

Then the Princess visited the giraffes.

"The giraffes have long necks," she thought as she watched them chomp tree leaves.

"They could raise the flag on my Royal Flagpole. Maybe they could be my friends."

But the giraffes
were too tall.
They did not want
a princess friend.

The Princess was sad.

Finally, the Princess visited the bears.

"The bears have sharp claws,"
she thought as she watched them dig in the dirt.

"They could peel fruit in my Royal Garden.
Maybe they could be my friends."

But the bears were too mean. They did not want a princess friend.

The Princess was sad.

Just as the Princess was about to leave, she felt something wet and slippery touch her hand.

It was a Penguin.

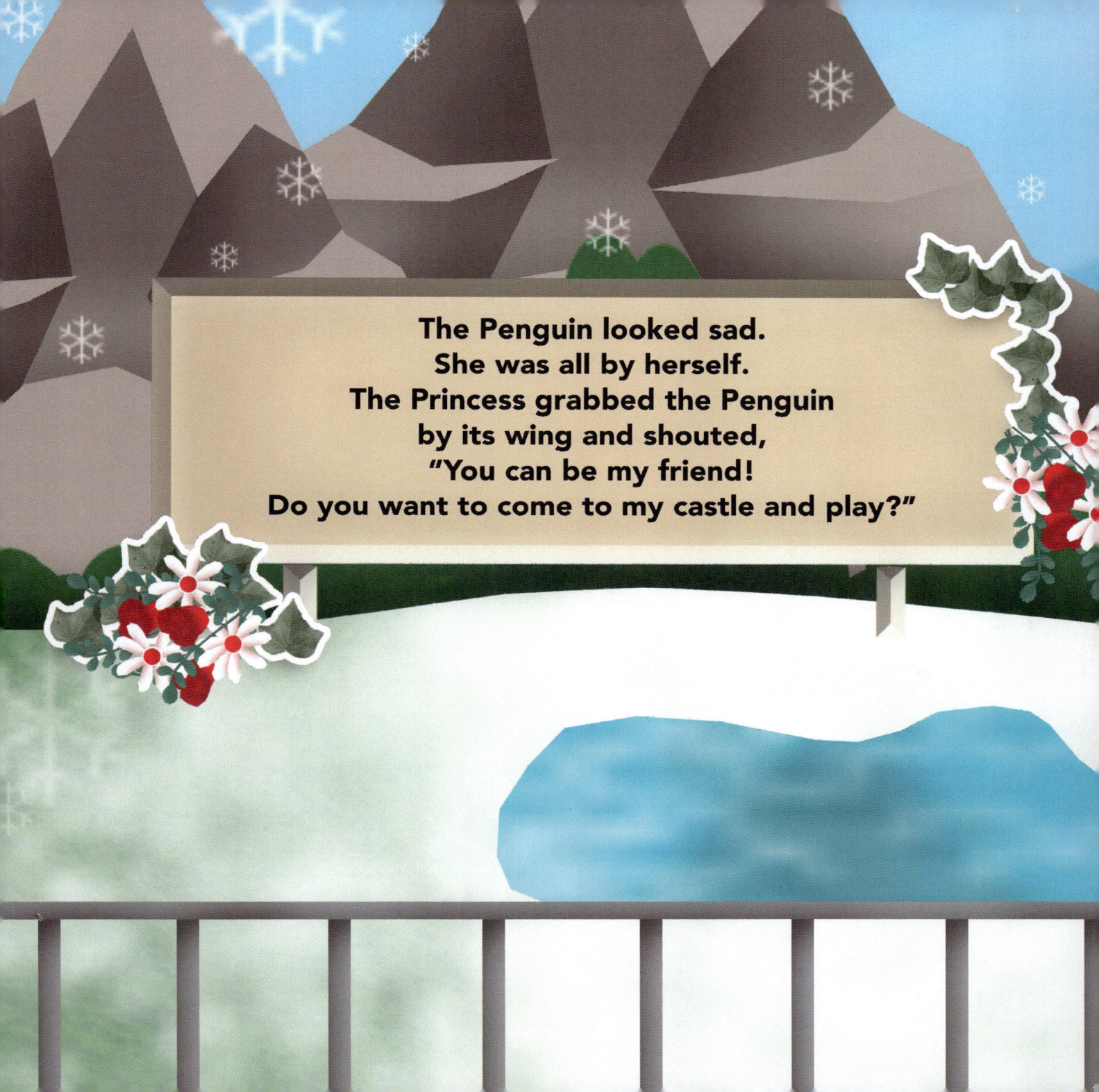

The Penguin looked sad.
She was all by herself.
The Princess grabbed the Penguin
by its wing and shouted,
"You can be my friend!
Do you want to come to my castle and play?"

The Penguin flashed a penguin smile, and nodded.

"Good then,"
The Princess said,
smiling in return.

She was happy.

Together they walked...
and waddled...
to the
Royal Carriage.

They rode in the Royal Carriage, through the Royal Kingdom towards the Royal Castle.

They were no longer lonely. They had each other.

When they arrived, they were ushered through the Royal Gates. The Princess rushed the Penguin inside.

The Princess first took the Penguin to her Royal Bedroom.

"Let's play with dolls!" The Princess exclaimed.

The Penguin tried, but the dolls kept slipping between her wings.

The Princess felt sad. She said, "You can't hold these dolls because you do not have fingers." The Penguin looked sad too.

"Wait. I have an idea!" the Princess shouted.

The Princess smiled and escorted the Penguin to the Royal Kitchen.

"Let's make a pizza!" The Princess exclaimed.

The Penguin tried, but spilled the sauce all over the princess's dress.

The Princess felt sad.

She said,
"You can't make a pizza because you don't have hands."

The Penguin looked sad too.

"Wait. I have another idea!" the Princess shouted.

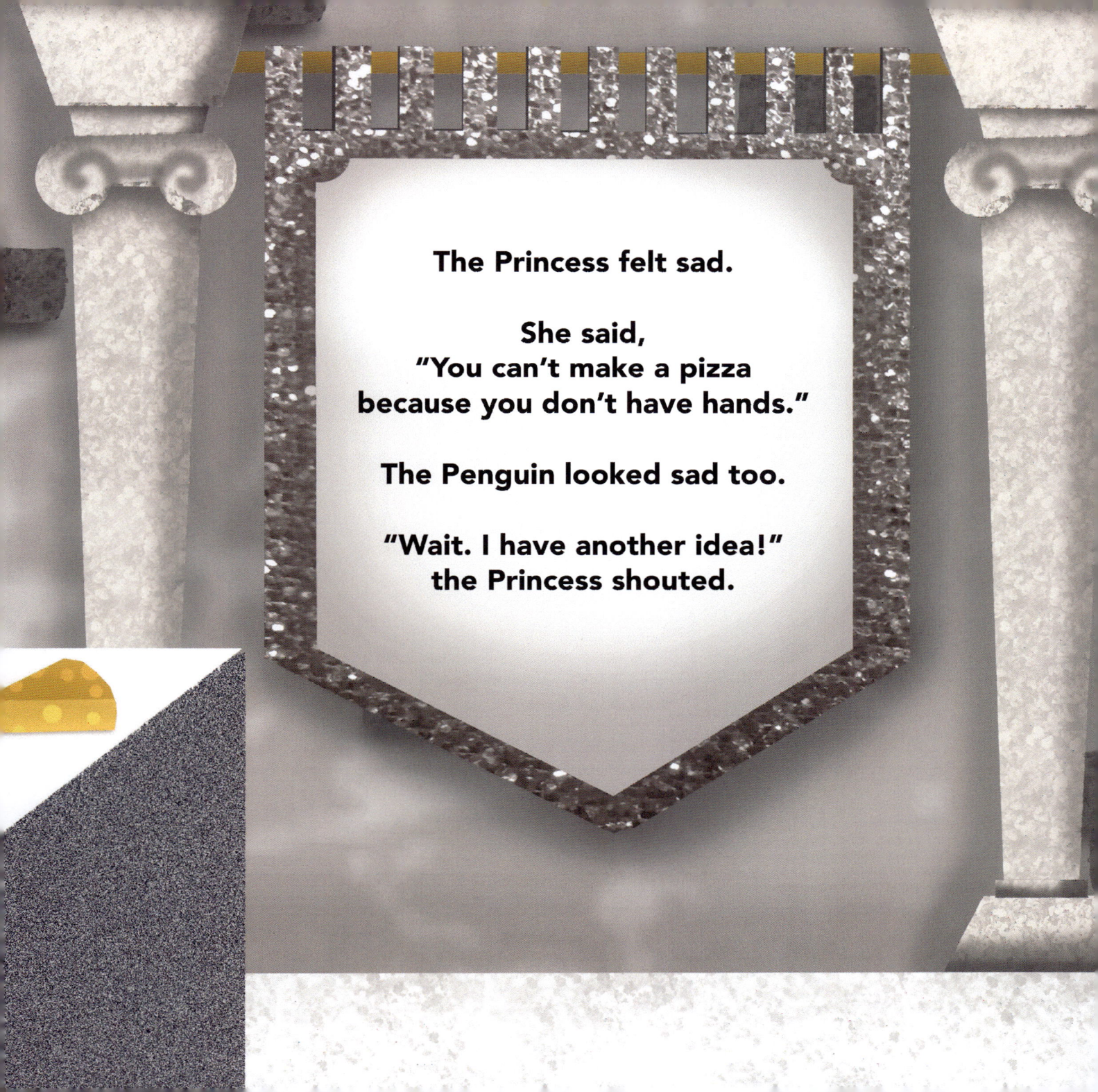

The Princess smiled and escorted
the penguin to the Royal Field.
"Let's run a race!"
The Princess exclaimed.
The Penguin tried, but she kept
tripping over her tiny feet.

The Princess felt sad. She said, "You can't run a race because you don't have feet." The Penguin looked sad too. "I don't have any more ideas. I do not think we can be friends," moaned the Princess.

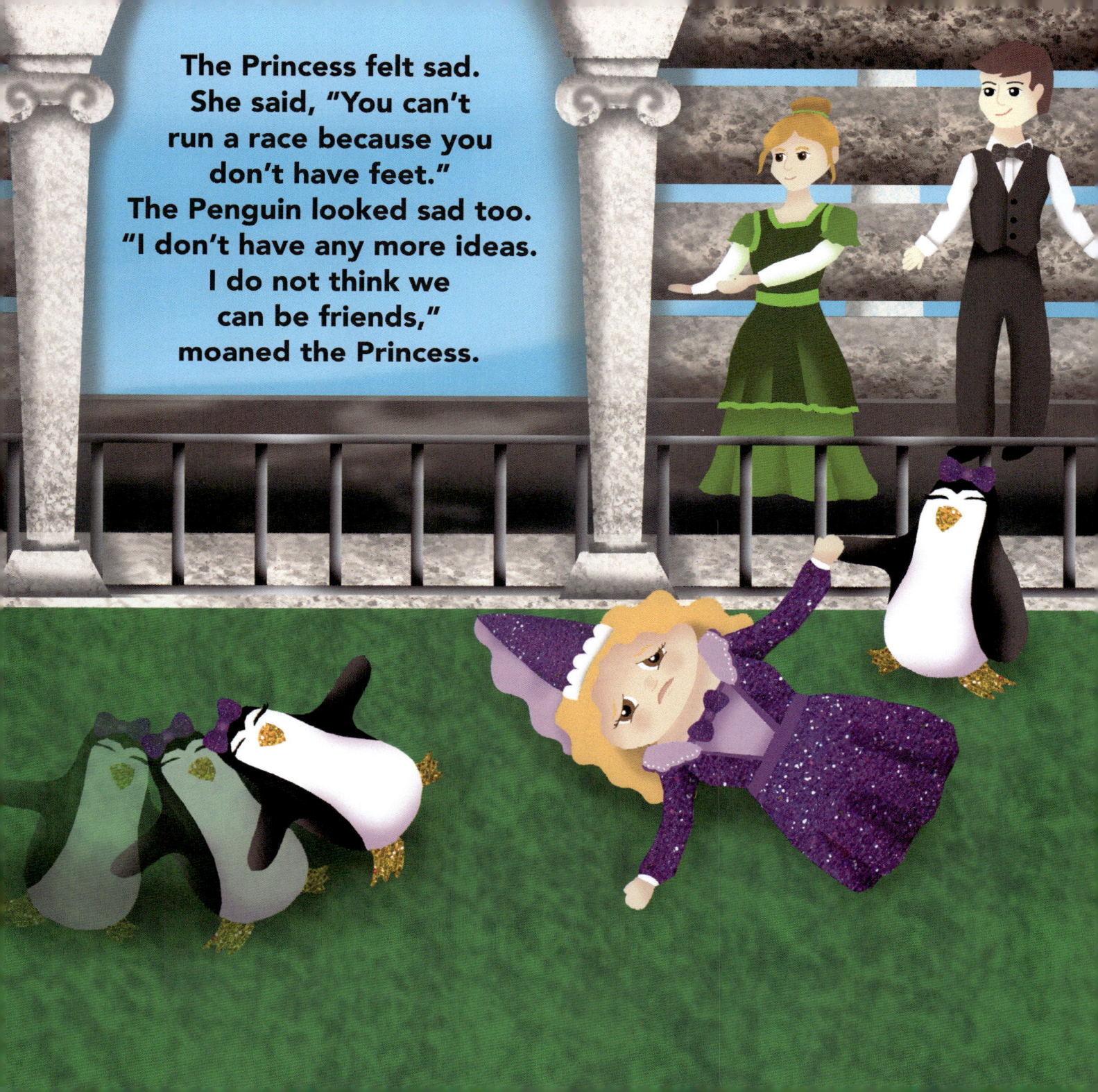

The Princess frowned and walked to the Royal Fountain, alone.

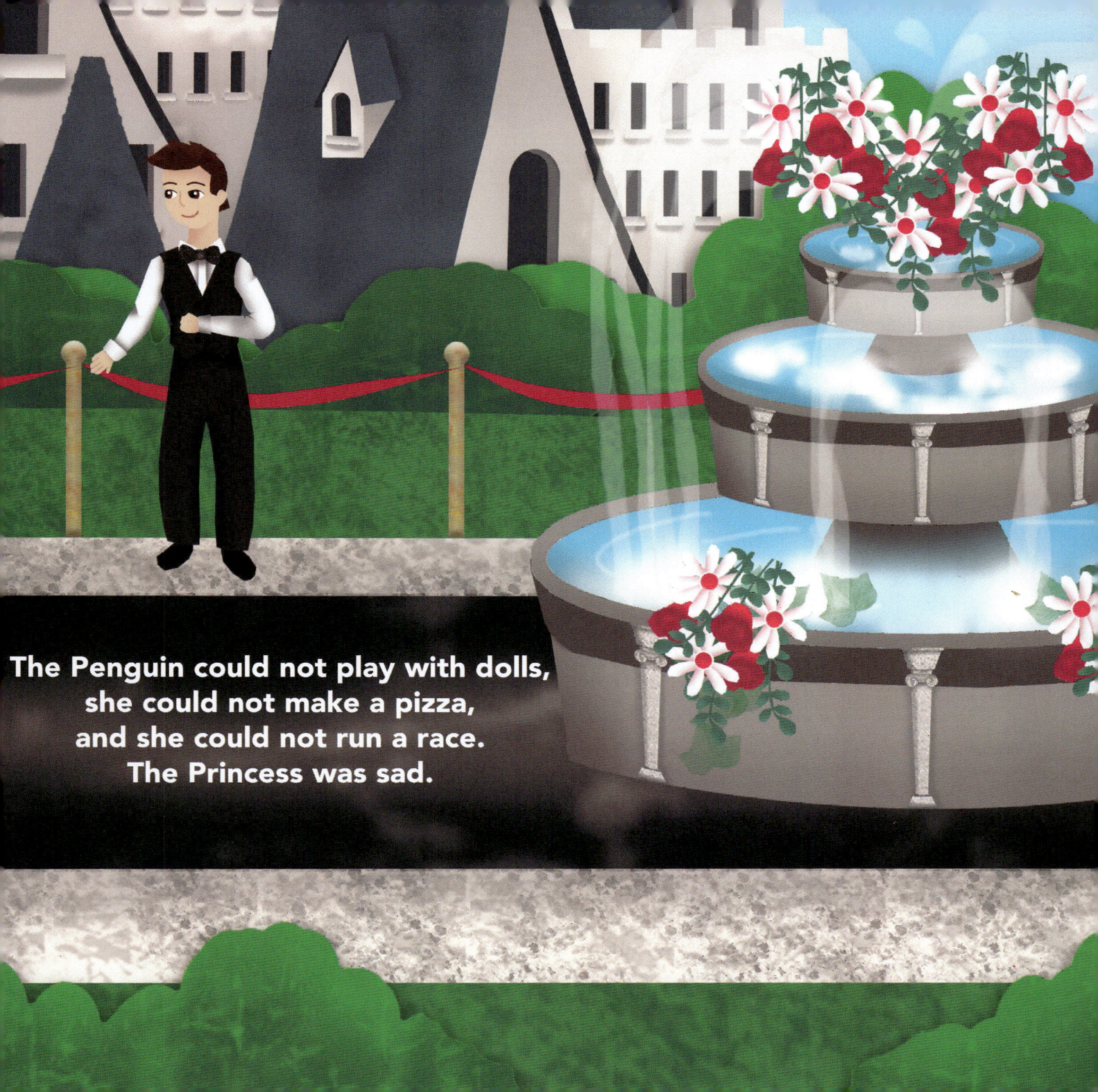

The Penguin could not play with dolls,
she could not make a pizza,
and she could not run a race.
The Princess was sad.

Suddenly, she heard a sound.

It was the Penguin, splashing in the fountain. The Princess smiled. "Now that's an idea!" She shouted at the top of her lungs.

The Princess jumped in the fountain.

The Princess and Penguin
swam and splashed
in the water, together.
They were happy.

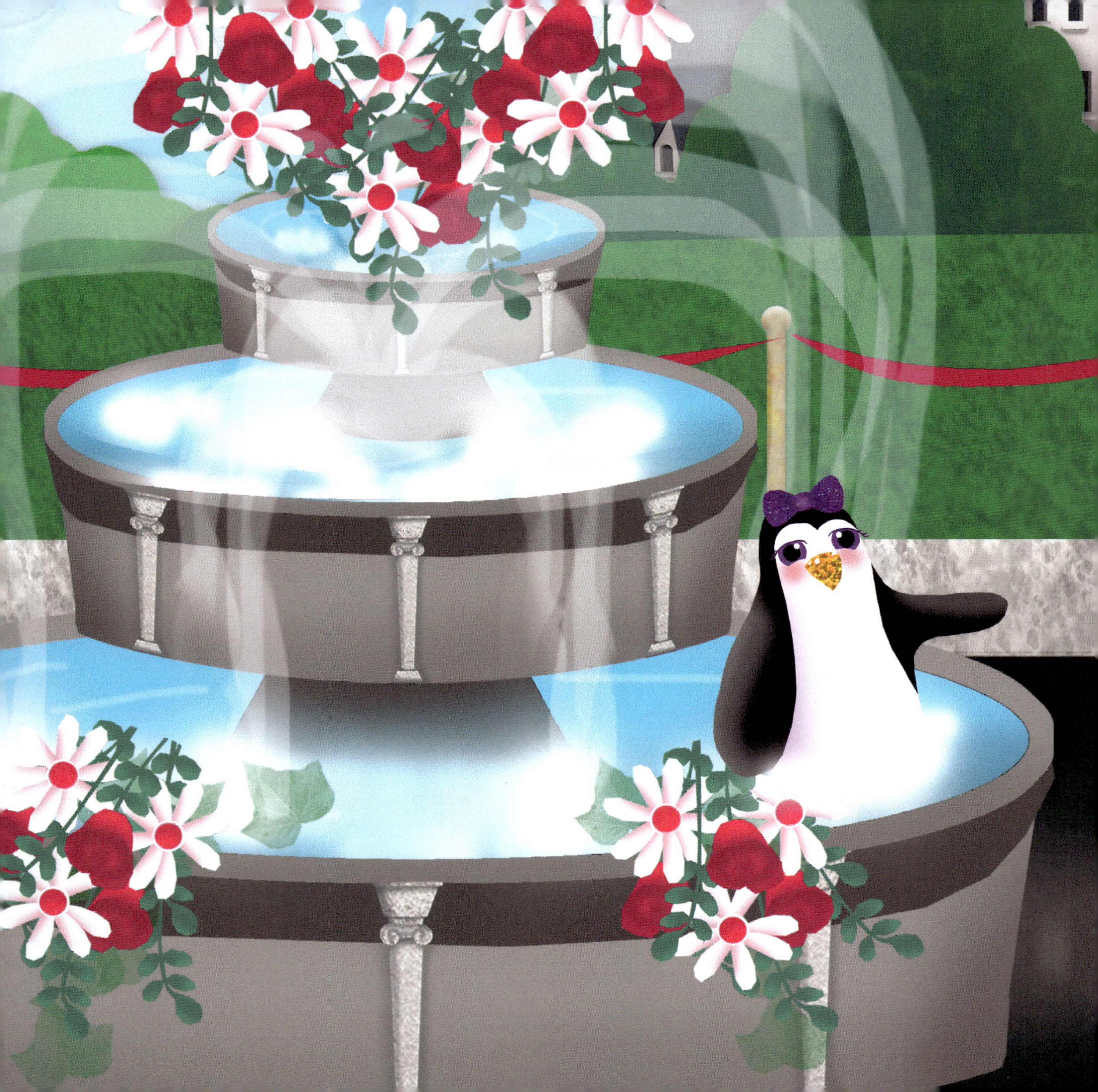

Then the Princess was cold.

"Wait. I have another idea!"
The Princess shouted.

The Princess smiled and escorted the Penguin to the Royal Mountain, covered in snow.

The Penguin smiled and raced down the mountain on its belly.

The Princess grabbed her Royal Sled and raced down the mountain as well.

ROYAL MOUNTAIN

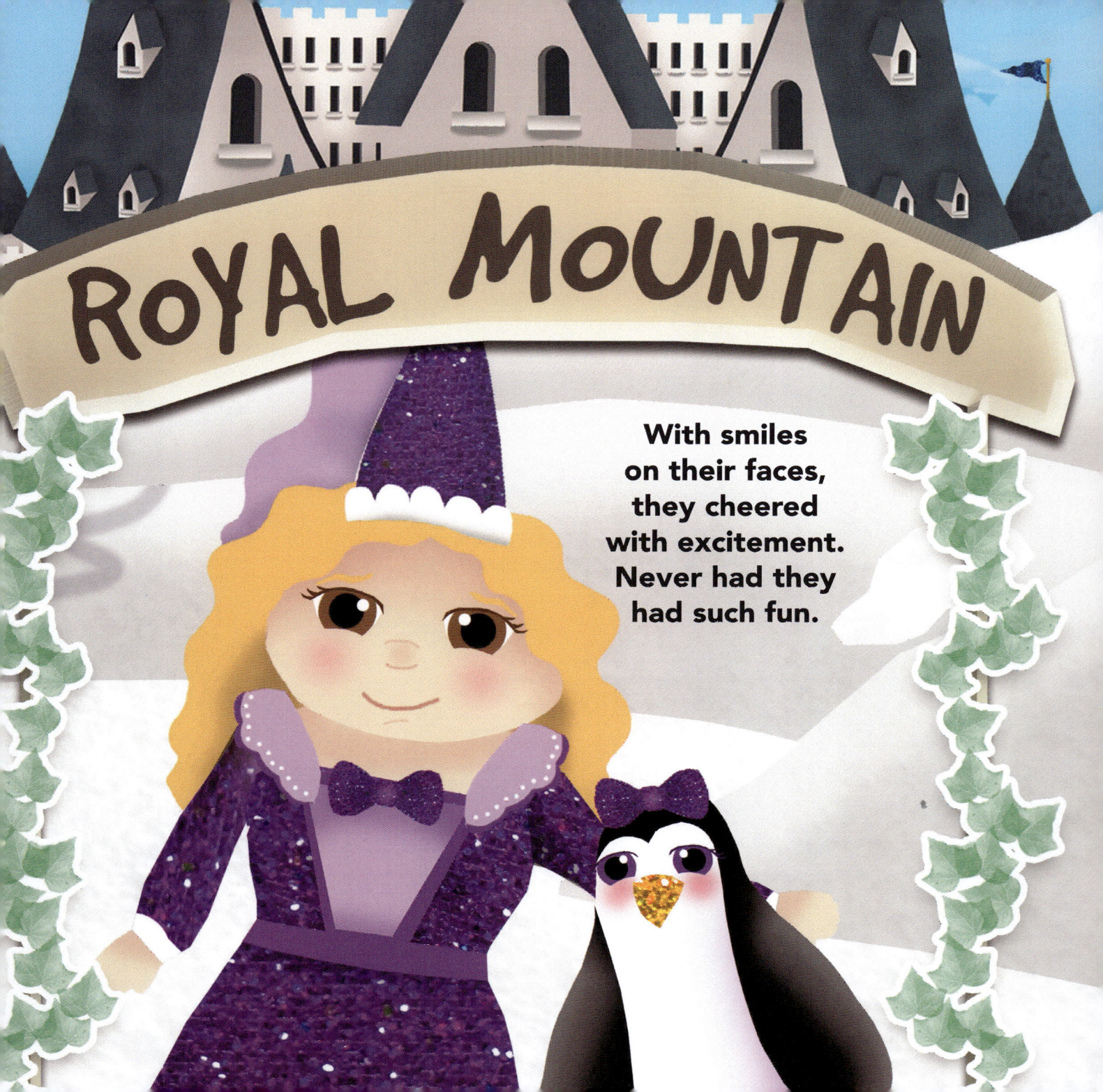

With smiles on their faces, they cheered with excitement. Never had they had such fun.

As the sun set, the Princess walked the Penguin to the Royal Carriage.

She hugged the Penguin tightly and said, "Being a good friend is not just about doing the things I like to do. It's about finding something we can both enjoy, together."

The Penguin nodded and smiled.

"Will you come back tomorrow?" The Princess asked.

The Penguin nodded and hopped into the carriage.

As the Royal Carriage rode out the Royal Gates, through the Royal Kingdom and back to the Royal Zoo, the Princess was so happy to make a Royal Best Friend.

Printed in Great Britain
by Amazon